•••••••••••••••••••••••••••••••

MEG
AND THE
GHOST OF
HIDDEN SPRINGS

•••••••••••••••••••••••••••••••

*MEG
AND THE
GHOST OF
HIDDEN SPRINGS*

ABOUT THIS BOOK

Meg stared at the shabby exterior of the once-beautiful Hannigan mansion, which had been the setting for a dark and mysterious tragedy long ago. "There's something scary about that old Hannigan house even in the daytime," Meg declared with a shiver, remembering that the house was said to be haunted.

Meg soon found out just how scary the Hannigan house could be, when a series of mysterious happenings began to occur. The apparition of a long-dead girl, ghostly footsteps, spectral tappings, strangely animated objects, a piano played by hidden hands, an unknown intruder—all lead Meg toward the solution of an exciting mystery in THE GHOST OF HIDDEN SPRINGS.

Meg

AND THE GHOST OF HIDDEN SPRINGS

by Holly Beth Walker

illustrated by Cliff Schule
cover illustration by Olindo Giacomini

® GOLDEN PRESS
Western Publishing Company, Inc.
Racine, Wisconsin

CONTENTS

1

THE HOUSE ON THE HILL

"There's something scary about that old Hannigan house even in the daytime, Uncle Hal," declared Meg Duncan with a shiver.

She stared across the river at a shabby mansion that rose like a gaunt ghost above the trees. Its majestic pillars, once gleaming white, were gray and peeling. The roof sagged at the corners, and one loose shutter banged forlornly in the wind.

The old house was said to be haunted.

"Do *you* believe in ghosts?" Meg asked suddenly, turning to her uncle.

That young man was seated with his back against the trunk of a tree, enjoying a sandwich from their picnic lunch. He looked around in surprise. "Ghosts, Maggie?" he echoed.

Meg's small oval face turned pink. "Well, people *have* been hearing strange sounds around that old place since Amelia Hannigan died," she insisted. "And the Carmody twins, Tim and Jim, swear they saw a spooky figure up there one night. It was right there—near the summerhouse."

Meg was half afraid her uncle was going to laugh at her, but he didn't. He tossed a crust of bread toward an eager squirrel.

"No, I don't exactly believe in ghosts, Maggie," he said slowly. "But I don't disbelieve in them, either. For as long as I can remember, folks around Hidden Springs have talked of seeing the ghost of little Kathleen Hannigan up there. And she died long before you and I were born."

Meg's dark eyes grew wide with awe. This was the first time she had heard that the ghost had a name. "Who was she, Uncle Hal?" she asked.

"I'm not sure, but I think she was old Amelia Hannigan's sister. People around Hidden Springs never liked to talk about it much, but some terrible tragedy happened near that house years and years ago.

"When I was your age, Maggie," he went on, "nobody lived there. Your mother and I used to

14

ride past the gates and imagine all sorts of spooky things. If it was dark, we'd put our horses to a gallop, to get away from there fast." He laughed at the memory.

Harold Ashley was a brother of Meg's mother, who had died some years before. He now lived in Washington, our nation's capital, where he worked for a museum. He was unmarried. And he had the gift of making an adventure out of everything he did—and of sharing those adventures with others. Meg was his favorite niece. And she adored him.

Uncle Hal often drove down to Hidden Springs to keep Meg company when her father had to be away. Today, however, he had come for a different reason—a reason related to the Hannigan house. He had come to take some photographs of the old mansion for his museum.

He looked up at the sun now, stretching his arms and yawning. Then he reached out and gave Meg's shining dark braid a playful tug. She had been staring again at the big house.

"Stop dreaming of ghosts, Maggie-me-love," said Uncle Hal. "We'd better be on the move and take those pictures while the light is good."

Meg blinked her eyes. Then she smiled back at

him. "Hand me your plate," she said.

Quickly she put the dishes and food back into the hamper. Then she jumped to her feet and brushed crumbs from her white blouse and blue jeans. Uncle Hal picked up the picnic basket, and Meg followed him to the car.

Uncle Hal loved old things. His car was an ancient Duesenberg, with a motor that purred like a sleek black cat.

He held the door for Meg as she jumped in. She leaned back against soft, red leather cushions.

It wasn't far to the big house—across a bridge and up a dusty lane. The great iron gates had been standing open since old Amelia Hannigan's death. They sagged now on rusty hinges, and Meg's uncle drove through them and parked the car.

Meg remembered the last time she had seen the owner of the gloomy mansion. Miss Hannigan had been a strange, eccentric character. She wore drab old-fashioned clothes, though she was said to be very wealthy.

She used to wander around the village, talking with the children. But she never would speak to the grown-ups.

One day Meg had been in the park with Kerry

Carmody, her best friend. Miss Hannigan came wandering up and sat near them on a bench. She began to ask them odd questions—all about their relatives. She wrote their answers in a little leather book.

Then Mrs. Partlow had come by, walking near the rose garden. She was an elderly neighbor of Meg's. At the sight of the other woman, Amelia Hannigan jumped up like a timid mole and scurried away.

What had she been afraid of? Meg wondered. And why had she lived in that lonely old house for so many years without making friends with her neighbors? Was it because of the mysterious tragedy Uncle Hal had spoken of?

These questions went through her head as she waited for her uncle to take out his camera. Uncle Hal's camera was an antique, too. It was old and fine and expensive. He carried it lovingly up the hill, with Meg close at his heels.

He told her more about the Hannigan mansion as he set up his camera and tripod. "This is the finest example of a plantation house left in Virginia, Maggie," he said. "It's a good deal more than a hundred years old."

"Who owns it now that Amelia is dead?" asked Meg with interest.

"One of her heirs, I suppose," answered her uncle. "I heard in Washington that some real estate people are trying to buy the property for a subdivision. That's why I was anxious to get down here and take my pictures. These fine old buildings sometimes disappear overnight. Men bring in bulldozers and push them down. They build modern uglies in their place."

While her uncle took pictures, Meg went exploring. She wanted to get a closer look at the summerhouse, where Tim and Jim had seen their "ghost."

It was a small building, open on three sides—gray and dilapidated, like the big house. In the sunlight, it looked deserted and harmless.

That loose shutter on the third-floor window of the house was still banging. Meg glanced up. A startled gasp escaped her lips.

The window was wide open, and a dingy curtain was billowing forth. That was funny. Meg was sure the window had been shut when she had seen it from across the river.

She turned to call down to her uncle. But the words never left her lips. A powerful gust of wind suddenly swept down the hill, blowing dust and leaves at her. It almost pushed her over.

On down the hill it rushed, buffeting Uncle Hal. Meg saw the heavy camera rise into the air. It seemed to twirl for a crazy instant. Then it crashed to the ground.

"Wow!" shouted Uncle Hal.

Meg went flying toward him. "Oh, I hope it isn't broken," she cried.

By now her uncle was picking up his precious camera. "No, it doesn't seem to be damaged," he said gratefully. "But that certainly was a freak wind. It was like a small tornado."

He turned to look at his niece, a rueful smile on his face. "I'm afraid the ghost of Hannigan House is warning us to get the heck out of here, Maggie," he said. "Luckily I got some good shots of the place." He put the tripod over his shoulder. "I should get back to Washington this afternoon, anyway."

As they started down to the car, Meg discovered that her heart was pounding with excitement. She completely forgot to mention that open window.

"Since you have to go right back to Washington anyhow, Uncle Hal," she begged, "will you drop me off at Kerry's house?"

Kerry lived on Old Bridge Road, just around the bend from Meg's home.

Uncle Hal obediently stopped the car before the Carmody gate. He got out and gave his niece a good-bye hug.

"I may be back in a day or two," he told her. "I want to get permission from the Hannigan lawyers to photograph the inside of the big house, too. Meanwhile," he added warningly, "you and Kerry keep out of trouble. I don't want you tangling with any unsavory ghosts."

He knew only too well how the young friends doted on mysteries.

Meg laughed. "We'll be careful, Uncle Hal," she promised. "Tell Mrs. Wilson I'll be home soon." Mrs. Wilson kept house for Meg and her father.

Meg waved at the gleaming black Duesenberg until it was out of sight. Then she turned and fairly flew up the walk to the Carmody's front door.

She couldn't wait to tell Kerry that she had visited the haunted house—and that she had learned the name of the Hannigan ghost.

2
SPOOKY TALK

The Carmodys lived in a wonderful old rambling house. There were seven children and even more pets. As Meg ran up the walk, two fat puppies came bounding out to jump against her legs. Excited as she was, she took time to give each one a friendly pat.

Nobody answered her knock at the door, but she could hear voices inside, so she pushed the door open and went in.

Meg was always welcome at the Carmodys'. She felt almost as much at home there as in her own house.

She followed the sound of the voices to the kitchen. The cook had made a huge batch of cookie dough. Most of the family were there—including Kerry and the twins. They were busily cutting out cookies.

Mrs. Carmody was rolling out the dough. Her hair was pinned back, and she wore an apron over her riding habit. She smiled at sight of the newcomer. "Hello, Meg," she said. "Get an apron and join us."

"Meggy! Meggy!" The two youngest children got down from their chairs. They came running to Meg, like the puppies. Their hands were all sticky, but she didn't mind. She hugged them warmly.

The twins were cutting out some strange, blobby-looking figures. Tim and Jim were thirteen, but they didn't seem the least bit ashamed to be caught making cookies with the younger children.

"We're making ghosts," declared Tim, holding one up for Meg to inspect. He plopped it down on the cookie sheet.

The twins looked almost exactly alike. They both had mischievous freckled faces and identical grins. Tim was the boldest.

"I'm making witches," said Kerry. "I'm going to decorate them. Come and sit here, Meg." She made a place for her friend at the big table. Then she turned to Meg, almost accusingly.

"Where were you all day?" she demanded. Kerry's pixielike face was puzzled beneath her cap of red-blond hair. "I called and called you." The two friends

played together almost every day.

"Just wait till you hear!" Meg could contain her exciting news no longer. "I've been up to the haunted house with Uncle Hal. We had a picnic, and he took some photographs of the house. It really is a spooky old place."

Her eyes grew darker as she remembered that mysterious gust of wind that had blown down from the hill.

"Did you see the ghost?" demanded Jim.

The twins were seldom serious. But whenever they spoke about the ghostly figure they had seen near the Hannigan house, their faces seemed to grow pale beneath their freckles.

"No, I didn't," Meg admitted. "But there is surely something funny going on around there." She told them about the window that had opened when she wasn't watching.

"I'm positive it was closed when Uncle Hal and I had our picnic," she said. "He told me that people have been seeing a ghostly form around the Hannigan place for years and years. A terrible tragedy happened up there long ago, when a young girl died. Uncle Hal called her 'little Kathleen.' "

"Maybe that's who the twins saw," whispered

Kerry, her blue eyes wide. Nobody had quite believed the twins' strange story when they first told it. Now Kerry looked at her brothers with new respect.

"We sure saw something," said Jim solemnly. He stood up and gave his mother a sheet of cookies to put in the oven. "It was last Saturday night. We were coming home on our bikes from Scout meeting. You remember, it was raining—"

"First we saw a light up there," Tim interrupted his brother. "Then we saw that—that phantom, near the summerhouse. It looked like a thin girl. She had a kind of veil over her head—"

"And she was just sort of floating along in the rain—toward the riverbank—"

Meg found herself holding her breath.

Then Mrs. Carmody slammed the oven door. She had just taken out a pan of luscious-smelling cookies.

"I doubt if you boys saw a ghost," she said crisply. "But there was some mystery about the death of Amelia Hannigan's younger sister. I remember when I was a girl, I used to beg my grandmother to tell me about it. But she always clammed up and wouldn't talk—"

"That's exactly what Uncle Hal said!" exclaimed Meg. "He said Kathleen's death was tragic in some

25

way, but he didn't know much about it, either.''

"Oh, I wish we could find out what really happened," cried Kerry.

Mrs. Carmody placed a big tray of the fresh cookies on the table before the children. She asked Kerry to fetch glasses and a pitcher of milk.

Kerry jumped up promptly to obey.

"Now that Amelia Hannigan is dead," said her mother, "there's only one person left in Hidden Springs who might know the answer to that old mystery."

"Who's that?" asked Meg eagerly.

"Our neighbor, Meg—old Mrs. Partlow. Her family has lived around here since the beginning of time, I guess. She's president of the Historical Society, you know, and can tell you about most anything that ever went on around here."

Meg looked at Kerry. Kerry looked at Meg. But before they could speak, the telephone rang.

It was Mrs. Wilson, wanting to speak to Meg, to ask her to come home. "Remember, you have to do your ballet exercises before dinner," the housekeeper reminded her. "Your lesson is on Friday."

Meg was reluctant to go, but Mrs. Carmody wrapped some of the cookies in a napkin for her to take home. Kerry followed her friend out the door.

"Let's go tomorrow," she suggested in a whisper.

Meg nodded. The same idea had been in her own mind. "I'll ask Mrs. Wilson to make one of those yummy lemon cakes Mrs. Partlow likes," she whispered back. "Then we'll have an excuse to call."

Mrs. Wilson was delighted to make the cake. She and her husband, who did the gardening at the Duncan home, were very fond of motherless Meg. Meg's father worked for the government and was away from home a great deal. The kindly Wilsons took excellent care of his daughter.

Mrs. Partlow lived on the corner between Meg's house and Kerry's. She was an aristocratic old lady, so the two girls were dressed in their best clothes when they went to visit her the next day. They walked past the ancient walnut trees in her front yard, and at exactly three o'clock they knocked on her door.

"Meg and Kerry! How nice of you to call on me!" Mrs. Partlow was genuinely pleased to see them and accepted the cake in her gracious manner. Then she led them to a small sitting room.

Mrs. Partlow asked all the polite questions. How

was Meg's dear father? And how were Kerry's parents? Then she pointed out the portraits on her wall, as she always did. She began to tell stories about her famous ancestors.

Meg could hardly keep from fidgeting. She didn't care a fig about the ancestors, but she couldn't be rude and interrupt. Fortunately impulsive Kerry was not so patient.

"Mrs. Partlow," she finally burst out, "we came to ask you some questions. Mother says you know everything about Hidden Springs. Can you tell us how Kathleen Hannigan died?"

"Kathleen Hannigan!"

Mrs. Partlow always sat very straight. Now she became absolutely rigid. Meg could see that she was very much upset by Kerry's question.

"You know my brothers, Tim and Jim," Kerry went on quickly. "They saw something odd near the old Hannigan house. They even thought it might be a—a *ghost*."

She stammered a little, under the elderly woman's cold blue stare.

Mrs. Partlow looked thoughtfully at her two young visitors. Then, to Meg's relief, she seemed to relax.

"So little Kathleen is walking again," she said.

She sighed softly. "It's a very sad story, girls, and it happened long ago. I suppose Hidden Springs has outlived the shame of it now, and there's no harm in telling it."

Meg and Kerry were more mystified than ever by those strange words. Meg felt a little chill curl along her spine. Did old Mrs. Partlow really believe in the ghost of Kathleen Hannigan? She wondered.

What could have happened that was so terrible that nobody had wanted to talk about it?

3
ROSES FOR KATHLEEN

Before she would tell them her story, Mrs. Partlow ordered tea for her young guests. She served it with the delicious lemon cake they had brought.

Meg was much too curious now to care about tea and cake. But she accepted them politely.

"Did you know Kathleen Hannigan, Mrs. Partlow?" she asked.

"I saw her many times," the old lady replied. "She was a friend of my older sister, Helen. They both went to Miss Perkins's private school. Kathleen was about fifteen when her family came here from New York. I was only five."

"What really happened to her?" demanded Kerry impatiently. "And why did the Hannigan family move away?"

Mrs. Partlow looked quite distressed. "I'm almost ashamed to say it, Kerry," she admitted, "but I'm afraid the good people of our town drove them away."

At this, the two girls could only stare.

"You see, this all happened not too long after the turn of the century," Mrs. Partlow continued. "There were still many people in the South who were suspicious of northerners—especially wealthy ones. Mr. Hannigan was said to be a millionaire, and he spent a fortune restoring the plantation house, which was in ruins when he came. It was a beautiful sight when it was finished," she added, "sparkling white among the trees—with acres of flowering shrubs around it."

Meg set her cup quietly on the table and leaned forward to listen.

"The family had three children: a small boy named Collin; Miss Amelia, the eldest daughter, who was quite a homely girl; and little Kathleen. Mrs. Hannigan was a friendly person who wanted to become part of the community, but people around here called her a social climber. They felt bitter because the Hannigans had bought the old plantation house."

"I should think they'd be pleased," remarked Meg

with a frown. "After all, they saved it from ruin."

"Well, they weren't pleased. The ladies of Hidden Springs didn't call on Mrs. Hannigan. They didn't invite her to their homes. In fact, they quite ignored the newcomers—except for little Kathleen. She was such a bright, happy girl that people couldn't help but smile when they saw her on the street.

"Because Kathleen was so popular, Mrs. Hannigan decided to give her a party on her sixteenth birthday. It was to be a big affair, with butlers and fine foods and musicians from the city. All the important people in town were to be invited, including my own sister. . . ."

Mrs. Partlow paused. Again that pained look crossed her face. "The night came. It was a stormy night, but the great house shimmered with lights. The doors were open, and music was playing. It was a costume party, and the family, dressed in their expensive clothes, stood near the door—waiting for the guests to arrive."

Again the speaker paused. "The hours went by— one by one—and nobody came."

"Nobody?" echoed Meg in dismay. She was shocked by the cruelty.

"Nobody. Afterward, the servants told what had

happened. When the Hannigans realized that no one in town had accepted their invitations, the music was stopped, and the musicians were sent away. Then little Kathleen began to cry. She ran out of the house.''

There was a lump in Meg's throat, and tears had gathered in Kerry's blue eyes.

"And then what happened?" Meg asked softly.

"She ran up the hill to that little summerhouse," said Mrs. Partlow. "She was sobbing as if her heart would break. Her poor father ran after her, to comfort her. But she wouldn't be comforted. She broke from his arms and ran toward the riverbank—"

"And then . . . ?" whispered Meg, dreading to hear the rest.

"The ground was slippery from the rain," said their hostess. "Kathleen must have fallen over the bank. When her father reached her, he found her with her face in the water. She had struck her head on a rock and drowned."

For a moment, Meg couldn't speak. She had never imagined anything like this.

"Then weren't the people around here sorry?" she asked.

"Yes, indeed." Even Mrs. Partlow's eyes were

misty. "The girls who loved Kathleen were very angry. My sister accused our Aunt Martha, who was quite snobbish, of tearing up her invitation. Nobody ever wanted to talk about that night again. Those who had snubbed the Hannigan family wouldn't even tell if they had been invited or not."

Mrs. Partlow poured herself another cup of tea. "Kathleen Hannigan was buried in the cemetery behind the old church."

She pointed through the window toward the spire of the historic village church. "People tried in every way to be kind."

"When it was too late," put in Meg sadly.

"Yes. They sent flowers and called, but they were all turned away. The day after the funeral, the Hannigan family simply left town. They left the house exactly as it was—the tables set with silver and china, flowers in the vases. Kathleen's father declared that the old place could rot on its foundations before the Hannigans would return."

"But Miss Amelia did come back," said Kerry.

"Yes, many years later, after her parents had died. But she never became friendly with the neighbors. We all tried hard to make her feel welcome, but nothing helped."

Mrs. Partlow was plainly unhappy about it. It was hard for her to admit that her proud village had been in the wrong. "Ever since that terrible night," she added, "people have thought they could see the ghost of Kathleen around that old summerhouse."

"Did you ever see her, Mrs. Partlow?" asked Meg.

Mrs. Partlow smiled. "Not exactly, Meg," she answered. "But I used to hear her—at least, I imagined I did. That is an odd little summerhouse. The winds whip around it in a peculiar way. When I was your age, my friends and I used to creep under the fence and go there sometimes. We'd listen at the back of that little building. Sometimes we thought we heard the sounds of someone sobbing."

Meg's face grew thoughtful. She didn't quite believe in ghosts, but it seemed more likely than ever that there just might be one around the Hannigan mansion.

"She was a beautiful girl, little Kathleen," Mrs. Partlow went on. "She had thick, dark hair and big, long-lashed eyes the color of violets. I think I have a picture of her somewhere in the attic, taken at Miss Perkins's school."

"Oh, could we see it?" begged Kerry.

"Why not? If I can find it, that is."

The girls followed Mrs. Partlow up the stairway to the attic. It was filled with the castoffs of several lifetimes, though everything was neatly stored. In an old trunk, Mrs. Partlow came upon a velvet-covered album.

The picture was of a group of young ladies standing before a magnolia tree. The face of Kathleen stood out among the rest—big-eyed, smiling, lovely.

Meg and Kerry looked at it for a long time.

They were very quiet as they bid Mrs. Partlow good-bye. It had been a strange story, indeed, and a tragic one. As they came out into the street, Meg again spied the church spire through the trees.

"Let's go see if we can find her grave, Kerry," she suggested.

"All right. Then let's change our clothes and get our bikes. We can ride up to the Hannigan house and look around—if you dare." Kerry's small, impish face was full of challenge.

Meg knew exactly what Kerry wanted to do: the very thing she herself was tempted to do. Could the ghost of poor Kathleen still be heard crying in the summerhouse?

Meg and Kerry had visited the quaint cemetery many times before. Some of their ancestors were buried there. They came upon the familiar names of Ashley and Jackson on the weathered tombstones.

It was Kerry who spied the grave of Kathleen.

"There it is," she called softly, pointing to a white marble stone. "H-a-n—Hannigan!" They both ran toward it.

Guarding the stone, with outspread wings, was a carved angel. On the mossy stone was the name they sought—KATHLEEN—and the dates of her birth and death.

But that was not what caught Meg's eye. "Look, Kerry," she gasped. "Someone else has been here already today!" She pointed down.

There, on the grassy mound, somebody had placed a sheaf of roses.

Meg bent to touch them. They were all as red as blood—and as fresh as spring.

4
A REAL LIVE GHOST

"Who would put fresh flowers on an old grave like this?" Kerry asked hollowly, looking across the mound at Meg.

Meg just shook her head. "I have no idea. There aren't many people alive who even knew Kathleen. And I'm sure there's more to her story than Mrs. Partlow told us," she added.

"Why would old Miss Amelia stay bitter all those years, after she came back to Hidden Springs, Kerry? She wasn't crazy—we know that. She was always kind and sensible when she talked to the kids on the street."

"That's right," Kerry agreed. "It was only the grown-ups she was mad at, I guess." The girls had started home now, to get their bicycles and change their clothes. "I wish there were some way we could get into that old house. We might find out what made Miss Amelia act so oddly."

Meg laughed. "That would be trespassing," she said sensibly. "But it would be fun."

Kerry had a hard time getting away from her little sister, Mary. Mary was a tagalong, and the girls didn't want to take her with them this time. Kerry finally sent her into the house for cookies, and they ran for their bikes.

They were soon wheeling down River Road toward the old Hannigan house.

Meg and Kerry parked their bikes inside the gates, where Uncle Hal had parked his Duesenberg the day before. They ran eagerly up the hill to the summerhouse. Kerry gave a little squeak as a squirrel ran past her feet.

Except for the squirrel, the place seemed deserted. They were breathless as they crept to the back of the summerhouse. They held their ears close to the grayed wall.

"Shhh!" Meg hissed as Kerry started to speak. Meg crouched motionless, straining every nerve to listen.

She heard a faint sound, as if coming from a great

distance. Then louder it came, a sound like a moaning sob. It grew and faded, again and again.

It might have been the wind, of course, sweeping through the sides of the summerhouse. Or it could have been a forlorn little ghost, sobbing mournfully because nobody came to her party.

Kerry looked at Meg. Her eyes were enormous. "It *does* sound like somebody crying—"

"*Boo!*" All at once, there came a scary yell from behind them.

Both girls whirled around. Meg's wide-eyed expression became an embarrassed little grin. Then she made a face at the newcomers.

The not-so-funny pranksters were the twins, Tim and Jim. They had followed the girls on their own bikes and sneaked up behind them.

Kerry wasn't amused. She was still shaking. "You had no right to scare us like that," she said crossly. "Mother told you never to jump at people."

The boys just laughed. "We knew you must be coming to see if you could find the ghost," Jim said. "Ghosts don't wander around in the daylight." The twins could act brave enough when the sun was shining.

"Maybe not," admitted Meg. "But you just listen

here." She told them the story of Kathleen Hannigan's tragic death.

The boys put their ears to the wall and listened. They were not impressed. "It's just the wind," said Tim. "We probably saw the real ghost. Let's poke around a little," he suggested to the others. "Amelia Hannigan was supposed to be rich. Maybe she dropped a few gold coins in the flower gardens."

Meg hesitated. She looked up at the third-floor window that had been open. It was now closed. She had the uncanny feeling that they might not be alone at the Hannigan house. Somebody—or something—might be inside.

By now the boys were on their way around the front of the house, followed by Kerry. Meg ran to catch up.

On the west side of the building, they made a discovery. The big doors covering the outside basement steps were lying open. The house was supposed to be locked up tight.

For a moment, the four stood there in silence, looking curiously down into the darkness.

"Let's explore a little, Jim," Tim said boldly.

His brother frowned. "We really shouldn't. It would be trespassing."

"Can't do any harm to take a look," Tim retorted. "We'll only take a minute." Without waiting, he started down the dim stairway. The brothers were seldom separated, and Jim was soon at his heels.

Meg and Kerry knelt at the sides of the opening and watched the boys disappear. Meg expected them to take one look and come right back, but they didn't. She could hear them prowling around among boxes and cans. There was the sound of a creaking door, followed by a slam—then nothing more for a long, long time.

"What are they doing?" asked Kerry nervously. "Father is going to be furious with them for going into somebody else's house."

"I don't know what they're up to," Meg answered, feeling annoyed, "but I'm going to find out."

She ventured a few steps down the stairs and paused to look around. A cobweb floated against her cheek, and she slapped it away. For a moment, she couldn't see, but her eyes soon got used to the darkness. She went a few steps farther. Kerry was close behind her.

Meg could now see another door at the far end of the basement. She remembered that some of the old plantation houses had wine cellars.

"Jim . . . Tim!" she called out anxiously.

Then she heard the boys. Their voices came from behind the door. They began to pound on it, shouting at the same time.

"Help! Meg, help us! We're locked in here. Let us out!"

Both Meg and Kerry went forward then. They had to pick their way among boxes and trunks. Meg pulled at the handle of the door. To her dismay, she found that it wouldn't open.

"It slammed shut after us," came Tim's voice in muffled tones. "Hurry up with that door. It's pitch-dark in here."

"I can't get it open," Meg shouted back. "But don't worry. We'll go for help. We'll bring Constable Hosey."

Meg and Kerry scrambled back up the cellar stairs. Constable Hosey was the law officer in Hidden Springs. More than once he had helped Meg and Kerry out of difficulties. They, in turn, had helped him solve a few of his cases.

Meg dashed around toward the front of the big house. She was so anxious to bring help for the twins that she didn't watch where she was going.

Suddenly she crashed head on into another running figure—one in just as much of a hurry as she was.

Meg backed away in alarm. The other person was an older girl—about fifteen, Meg guessed. She seemed to have come from the house.

She had a terrified expression on her face. But she wasn't half as scared as Meg was when Meg got a good look at that face. It was the face of Kathleen Hannigan—the girl whose picture Meg had seen at Mrs. Partlow's!

For one instant, Meg thought she was truly seeing a ghost—a real, live ghost.

The girl didn't speak. She just gave Meg one horrified stare from those great violet blue eyes, then ran on, vanishing around the corner of the house.

"Who was that?" cried Kerry, from behind Meg.

"I don't know," Meg answered in a dazed voice. "But I'm sure she ran out of the house. See—the door is still open. Let's get out of here quick," she added, "and go get Constable Hosey to rescue the boys. I'm scared something will happen to them."

They were already on their way, flying like two frantic sparrows, down the hill to their bicycles.

As they rode off toward the bridge, Meg heard the

sound of a motor behind them. She looked around to see a small, dark car. It was just coming out through the big gates.

The car was driven by a dark-haired woman, and beside her sat the strange girl Meg had seen near the house. The car turned in the other direction. *It must have been parked behind the house all the time,* thought Meg.

She pedaled her bike faster than ever. If those people were living in the Hannigan house, they'd be mighty surprised to find two freckle-faced boys in their cellar.

5

A GIRL NAMED KATHLEEN

"Locked in the cellar, you say?"

Constable Hosey was annoyed when the excited girls came dashing into his office with their alarming news. It was six o'clock. He was just about to go home for supper.

"What in blazes are those pesky twins doing around that old house, anyway?" he demanded.

Meg and Kerry were breathless from their long ride. Meg took a deep breath. "The twins didn't mean any harm, Constable Hosey," she said defensively. "They were just looking around. Then that door slammed shut, and they couldn't open it."

"All right, Meg," said the constable. "I suppose we'll have to get them out. Come along and show me where they are." He led them toward his car.

"You can pick up your bikes later."

It was getting dark when the three arrived at the big house. And someone had been there before them. The cellar doors were closed and padlocked. There was no sign of the boys.

Meg was worried. "Maybe we can get down there from inside the house," she suggested. She had already told the constable about seeing the strange girl run from the house. "The door may still be unlocked."

"There's some funny business going on here," grumbled Constable Hosey as they went up the front steps. "After Miss Amelia died, I came here with Jenny Grayham—the woman who kept house for her. We closed the shutters and locked the place up tight. I sent the keys to the Hannigan lawyer. Isn't supposed to be anybody living here, far as I know."

Meg had guessed right. The front door was unlocked and ajar on its hinges.

Somewhat timidly she and Kerry followed Constable Hosey into a gloomy hallway.

The man reached up to snap on the light switch. Nothing happened. "I forgot—we had the electricity turned off," he said. Then he took out his flashlight.

A gleaming splotch of light bobbed against the wall.

Meg looked around curiously. Kerry pressed close against her and gripped her hand. There wasn't much to see. The great hall went all the way through the house. It was lined with dark portraits and mirrors. There was dust on the polished floor.

Constable Hosey knew the old house well. He went right to the kitchen, where a door led down to the cellar. Fortunately, it, too, was unlocked. He started down the steps.

"You kids stay here," he ordered as Meg and Kerry began to follow. "I don't want you getting hurt."

They sat close together at the head of the stairs, listening to the groans of the rafters as the ancient house settled for the night. "The door's right there in front of you," Meg called out.

Her voice sounded strange in the cavernous basement. She was praying the boys would be safe.

They were. As soon as Constable Hosey rattled the door handle, they began to yell.

"Help, help! Let us out of here."

"Hold your horses in there, boys," said the constable calmly. "This door won't budge. I'll have to get some tools and break the lock."

He went back to the police car for a hammer and chisel. It wasn't long before the two grimy boys stumbled out of their dark prison. They had been scared, all right, but there was a weak grin on each freckled face as they came up the steps.

Kerry was crying from sheer relief at seeing her brothers unharmed.

Meg was all business. "What happened?" she asked. "Did somebody lock you in?"

"We don't know." It was Tim speaking. His voice sounded puzzled. "We saw that door and thought we'd just take a peek inside. But a funny thing happened. When we came close to it, it just opened by itself."

"Like those magic-eye doors in the supermarkets," put in Jim. "Then when we got inside, it just slammed shut behind us."

"Did you get a chance to look around in there?" asked Meg eagerly.

"A little bit. Tim had his flashlight, but the batteries were weak. Before they finally went dead, we had a chance to look. It's an old wine cellar, all right. There were some dusty bottles on the racks—"

"And that isn't all," the other twin said excitedly.

"It was like a shop down there, Meg. There was a whole bunch of old radios, and wire and tools. And something that looked like a transmitter—"

"Tim thinks somebody might have been sending messages from this place. Maybe a secret agent . . . a spy—"

"Oh, that's just silly!" exclaimed Kerry. "Old Amelia Hannigan certainly wasn't any spy!"

Meg wasn't so sure it was silly. She wasn't surprised at anything about the old house now, including ghosts. "Did you see any more ghosts?" she asked with a little giggle.

The boys could laugh now, too. "No," said Tim. "But we did hear something funny. The fireplace wall ends down in that room. There's a dumbwaiter at one side of it—for carrying up bottles, I guess. When I was standing near it, I could hear noises from the other floors. I heard footsteps—"

"That's enough of this nonsense, boys." Constable Hosey had been standing below them, holding his tools. Now he came up the steps. "You twins get your bikes and get on home as fast as your legs will carry you," he ordered crossly. "You've caused enough trouble for one night. You're lucky I don't put you in jail for spoiling my supper."

The twins were soon out of the house and bounding down the hill to their bicycles. Meg and Kerry followed Constable Hosey to his car. He delivered them to their own doorsteps.

Mrs. Wilson was quite upset when Meg arrived, late for dinner and covered with dust.

"Where have you been, child?" she asked. "I called Mrs. Carmody and—"

Meg grinned. "I was helping Constable Hosey rescue the twins," she said. As briefly as possible, she explained the mysterious events of the day.

"My, oh, my!" Mrs. Wilson shook her graying head. "I've always heard that old Hannigan place was haunted, but I've never much believed in ghosts. Now, you get washed, Meg, while I warm up your dinner."

Meg had followed her into the kitchen as she told her story. Mr. Wilson was seated at the table. Usually quiet, he spoke up now.

"You and Kerry keep away from that old place," he warned Meg. "Might be a tramp hiding out in there."

Meg didn't sleep much that night. There were too many unanswered questions chasing through her

53

mind. What strange hand had closed the cellar doors? What was that girl doing in the house, and why had she been so frightened?

"Maybe the house belongs to those people," suggested Kerry the next afternoon. She and Meg were on their way to the village to pick up their bicycles. "They might have bought it."

Meg shook her dark head. "They can't be living there, because the electricity is off. And Constable Hosey never heard of them. What I'd like to know," Meg added, frowning, "is how come that girl looked so much like Kathleen—the one who died."

That was one question soon to be answered.

They were just passing the drugstore, and Kerry stopped suddenly. "Let's go in and have a soda," she said impulsively. "I got my allowance today. I'll treat." She jingled some coins in her pocket.

It was a hot day, and Meg was happy to accept. They were soon sitting at a front booth in the store, sipping tall, cool chocolate sodas.

All at once, Meg heard voices from the booth next to them.

"I don't want to go back there, Mother," a young voice was saying. "It's a horribly gloomy old place."

"But we have to go back, Kathleen." This was a woman's voice. "We promised that we would meet Mr. Carberry—"

Kathleen. Meg caught her breath at hearing the name.

"Excuse me, Kerry," she said tensely. "I'm going to get another straw." She slipped out of the booth and went to the soda fountain and got a straw. Then she turned slowly and looked at the two people in the other booth.

One was a dark-haired, middle-aged woman. Across from her sat a girl in her teens. Her eyes were half-shut as she looked down at her drink. Long black lashes made shadows on her creamy skin. Her hair was long and thick and dark.

As Meg stood frozen, the girl suddenly looked up and met her stare.

It could have been little Kathleen—Kathleen Hannigan, come back to life!

6
GHOSTLY FOOTSTEPS

The strange girl recognized Meg almost at once. A lovely smile spread over her face. Meg walked slowly toward her.

"Haven't we bumped into each other before?" the girl asked.

Meg laughed. "I'm afraid we have," she admitted. "I'm awfully sorry. I wasn't watching where I was going. And I didn't expect anybody to be near that old house."

The girl turned to the woman. "This is the girl I saw near Aunt Amelia's house yesterday," she said. "I'm Kathleen Martin," she told Meg, "and this is my mother, Mrs. Martin."

"I'm Meg Duncan." By now the curious Kerry was beside her. "And this is my friend Kerry."

Mrs. Martin smiled at the two girls. "I'm so happy to meet you," she said. "Perhaps you can help us. We're staying at the Lee Motel, near the highway. We don't know a thing about Hidden Springs. Won't you girls sit with us and have some ice cream?"

"We already have sodas," said Kerry. "I'll get them."

The next thing Meg knew, she and Kerry were sitting with the Martins, chatting about their favorite subject—the Hannigan mansion.

Meg was beginning to understand a lot of things. "You must be a relative of Amelia Hannigan," she said to Kathleen. "I heard you call her aunt—"

The girl nodded. "She was really my great-aunt. I saw her only once in my life."

Mrs. Martin spoke up. "I'm afraid Kathleen belongs to the poor branch of that family," she said. "Her grandfather was Collin Hannigan, Amelia's brother. He ran away from home when he was a boy and went to California. That's where Kathleen was born."

"I was named after Grandfather's sister," the girl remarked. "He loved her very dearly, and she died when she was just a girl. Grandfather never liked to talk about it."

Meg nodded. "We know all about it," she said.

"Oh, tell me, please."

Meg didn't want to tell her about the tragic party just then. That would hurt too much. "It happened on a rainy night," she said. "She fell from the river-bank and was drowned. You must be the ones who put the roses on her grave," she added suddenly. "We saw them there yesterday."

"Yes. We brought them for Aunt Amelia's grave, but we couldn't find it."

"That old cemetery isn't used anymore," Meg explained. "There's another one east of town."

"The other Kathleen was awfully pretty." Kerry had been waiting impatiently to speak. "We saw her picture—you look exactly like her."

"I do?" Kathleen's eyes brightened with interest.

Kerry nodded her blond head. "Do you own the big house now, Kathleen?" she asked. "Are you going to live there?"

For a moment, the girl looked confused. "I really don't know," she said. "Aunt Amelia's lawyer sent us the keys to the house and asked us to come to Hidden Springs."

"He's going to meet us at the house tomorrow and read us Amelia's will," said Mrs. Martin. "It seems Miss Hannigan was an eccentric old lady. She left the house to my daughter, with certain strings attached. Kathleen has to do some special thing to inherit the house. We don't know, as yet, what that is.''

''I'm not even sure I want the old place,'' retorted Kathleen. ''The first thing we heard when we came to town was that it was haunted. And—and I believe it is!''

Her mother laughed merrily. ''My daughter has a wild imagination, girls,'' she said. ''She sees spooks around every corner.''

''You can laugh, Mother,'' Kathleen said defiantly. ''But it wasn't funny. We went there yesterday just to look. I was on the second floor, looking at the rooms,'' she told the girls. ''Mother had already gone to the car. I was supposed to lock the doors. But when I started down the stairs, I heard something behind me.''

Again Meg saw that frightened look in the blue violet eyes.

''It sounded like footsteps—like somebody running. I looked around, and *nobody was there.*''

''Why, that's what the twins—'' Kerry started to speak. Meg put her finger to her lips. She looked straight into Kathleen's pale face.

"Did you *see* anything strange?" she asked.

"No, but that old place is full of awful sounds. When I got downstairs, I heard terrible noises in the cellar—howling and shouting."

It was Meg's turn to laugh—with relief. "Well, that was no ghost, Kathleen," she said. "That was Kerry's twin brothers yelling for help. Is that why you ran out of the house looking so scared?"

"That was just the last straw," Kathleen said. She managed a faint smile when Meg told how the boys had been trapped in the basement. "But I heard other mysterious sounds—tappings on the walls. And when I was in the dining room, a plate jumped right off the plate rail, just as if something had pushed it."

"There *is* supposed to be a ghost there," Meg said, "but it's a harmless one. It's the ghost of little Kathleen. People say they see her walking near the river. You wouldn't have to be afraid of her.

"I hope you do inherit the house, Kathleen," she added earnestly. "My Uncle Hal says it's a real treasure. The property is worth a lot of money."

"I couldn't bear to live in it," declared the girl with a shiver.

"You may not get the chance, dear," said her mother. "We'll find out more about the will tomorrow." She got up from her seat.

"Thank you, Meg and Kerry, for telling us about the house," she said with a smile, "and about the other cemetery. We'll get some flowers now for Amelia's grave. I hope we'll see you both again."

"I wish she had invited us to go with them tomorrow," said Kerry a little later. She and Meg had found their bikes behind Constable Hosey's office and were riding home side by side. "I'd like to see more of that house, and I'd like to know what the will says."

Meg didn't answer. She was thinking of those mysterious events in the Hannigan house—strange tappings, running footsteps, a plate that "jumped" from the plate rail. There had to be a sane reason for it all.

Kerry had to go home to sit with her little sister and brother while her mother went shopping. The moment Meg reached her own house, she went to the telephone.

"Do you mind if I make a long-distance call to Uncle Hal at the museum, Mrs. Wilson?" she asked.

"You may if it's important," said the housekeeper.

"It's important, all right," said Meg.

She was happy to find her uncle in his office. "To what do I owe this pleasure, Maggie?" he asked on hearing his niece's voice.

"Uncle—Uncle Hal—" Meg was so excited she stumbled over her words. "Remember when you said you wanted to take pictures inside the Hannigan house?"

"Yes, what about it?"

"Well, I think you can get in—tomorrow," said Meg, "if you can come. I met the new owner—or the one who *might* be the owner. Her name is Kathleen Martin."

She told him all that had happened.

"Whew!" Her uncle whistled softly over the telephone. "Sounds as though there might be a poltergeist under that old roof."

"Poltergeist?" Meg had heard the word, but she wasn't just sure what it meant.

"That's a German word, Meg. It means 'noisy ghost.' Maybe the ghost of Kathleen Hannigan doesn't want *your* little Kathleen in the house—so she's throwing dishes."

"Oh, Uncle Hal!" Meg knew he was teasing. "I

know it sounds silly. But do you think you can come?'' she asked anxiously.

"I'll try, Maggie. But I'll have to get permission. Can't just barge in, uninvited. How do I find the Martins?''

"They're staying at the Lee Motel near the highway. You can telephone them there, Uncle Hal.''

"I'll see what I can arrange,'' he answered.

"And, Uncle Hal?''

She took a deep breath, then asked boldly, "Do you think you could take along a helper?''

There was a chuckle at the other end of the line. "I'll see what I can do, Maggie. If these people are as nice as you say they are, there should be no problem.''

"*Two* helpers?'' Meg asked hopefully.

"I suppose you mean you and Kerry,'' said her uncle. "I might have known you two young sleuths couldn't rest till you solved the mystery of the Hannigan ghost.

"Very well, Meg. I'll call the Martins. If all goes well, I'll pick you and Kerry up tomorrow afternoon, to help me take some pictures of the house. Good night, honey.''

"Oh, boy!''

Meg hung up the receiver and made a graceful little pirouette on the polished floor. Then right away she took the phone down again and dialed another number.

Kerry Carmody wasn't going to believe this!

7

INSIDE THE MANSION

Harold Ashley and his two "helpers" drove out to the Hannigan house early the next afternoon. They were met at the door by Kathleen's mother.

Mrs. Martin had opened windows on the first floor. Now the house seemed less forbidding to Meg and Kerry.

Meg introduced her uncle, and Mrs. Martin greeted him warmly. "We are delighted to have you take pictures," she said. "Do come in."

"I'm afraid I must confess that these girls came to look at the house," said Uncle Hal, flashing his winning smile. "They aren't much good as photographers, but they have been curious ever since Kerry's brothers supposedly saw that 'ghost' near the summerhouse."

"They are most welcome. My daughter was quite taken by your niece."

Kathleen appeared just then, dressed in pretty playclothes of a bright blue. They made her eyes seem bluer than ever.

She grabbed Meg's hand and motioned to Kerry. "Just wait till you see the ballroom—or drawing room—whatever it's called."

She seemed to have forgotten her fear of the day before. She was quite as thrilled as Meg and Kerry to explore the old mansion that might soon be hers.

The drawing room was just off the hall. It was an enormous room, with a high ceiling. There was a huge fireplace with a wooden mantel.

Meg and Kerry stood at the door and simply stared, openmouthed. Except for a faint layer of dust on the floor, the room sparkled. Dozens of small gilt chairs stood as if in waiting.

"I can't believe it," said Meg in awe. "The outside of the house is so shabby. Why would Miss Amelia keep this room so perfect?"

"I have no idea," said Kathleen. "But look there—" She pointed to a huge portrait above the fireplace. The other girls walked toward it. "That is a picture of the sisters, my great-aunts. And the

little boy is my own grandfather, Collin Hannigan.''

Meg held her breath. It was a beautiful picture. The older girl, Amelia, was seated. At her knees was a small blue-eyed boy. Standing behind them was Kathleen herself!

"It's uncanny!" Uncle Hal had come into the room with Mrs. Martin. "Except for her modern clothes," he said, "your daughter might have sat for that portrait herself. And that fireplace! It's a gem. Hand me my gadget bag, Meg.''

Uncle Hal didn't really need Meg and Kerry. So while he took his pictures, the two girls explored the house with Kathleen.

They found another surprise in the dining room. Tables were set with fine china and huge punch bowls, recently polished. This room, too, was in perfect order—as though guests might walk through the door at any moment.

The second floor of the house was dark and gloomy, because the shutters were closed. Here, except for a single room, everything was in a state of neglect.

That one room was spotlessly clean. Kathleen ran to open the windows and shutters. "I didn't see this the other time," she said.

Meg and Kerry gasped. "It must have been *her* room," Meg said in a whisper. "Kathleen's."

The four-poster bed had a canopy of ruffles. The carpets were rich and deep, the mirrors gleaming. Across the bed lay a party gown of exquisite pink satin, with a billowy skirt and a tiny waist.

Meg touched the dress with the tips of her fingers. It had been kept clean, but it was slightly faded, and there were traces of water marks on it.

"That must be hers, too," said Kathleen, coming back from the window. A little shudder went through her. "Do you suppose it was the dress she wore . . . that night?"

Meg couldn't answer. It seemed gruesome, some-how, to keep it like that—as if the young owner of the gown would step up any minute, to dress for her party.

"Your Aunt Amelia was strange, Kathleen," Meg said thoughtfully. "She was very kind, but she sel-dom went out of the house. When she did, she always seemed scared of something."

"I wonder what it was," said Kathleen.

Her mother appeared at the door. "You'd better come downstairs, dear," she said. "It's almost two-thirty. The lawyer should be here any minute."

Kathleen started off obediently, Meg and Kerry behind her. Meg paused in the hall.

"May I look around a little more?" she asked. "I'll be down in a minute, Kerry."

She wanted to be alone. She was curious about the room across the hall. She felt sure it had belonged to Miss Amelia. Perhaps it contained some clue to that strange woman's secret.

"Go ahead and look," said Kathleen cheerfully. "But watch out for spooks. Come on, Kerry."

Meg laughed. So far, the poltergeist had been very quiet. She crossed the hall to the other room— a twin to the one she had just seen. But what a contrast!

Everything in it was shabby. The curtains were faded; the carpets worn. This room had a four-poster bed, too, but the furniture had not been polished in years.

Meg stood in the center of the room, looking around her curiously. A heavy feeling of sadness came over her. She felt strongly the presence of the homely old lady who had lived there.

Questions beat on Meg's brain. All those years Amelia had kept her dead sister's room in order. Yet her own was an unbelievably dreary place.

70

There were two large window seats, covered with faded cushions, and, off in one corner, a huge old-fashioned rolltop desk. Meg walked over to the desk and slid back its lid. The desk, like everything else in the room, looked neglected. Papers and envelopes, many yellowed with age, were jammed into crowded compartments. Feeling a bit guilty but even more curious, she reached out to open one of the many small drawers at the back of the desk. As she did so, several sheets of paper in the too-crowded drawer caught at the top of the drawer opening. One particularly yellowed sheet fluttered to the desk top.

Feeling more and more like an intruder, Meg began to straighten the contents of the desk drawer. As she replaced the sheet that had fallen, a familiar object in the drawer caught her eye. It was the little notebook she had seen in Amelia's hand the day she had talked with Kerry and Meg in the park.

Feeling guilty, Meg removed it and began to glance through it.

There were some names scattered through the pages, including hers and Kerry's. Then a single phrase seemed to leap at her: *all those invitations*.

Meg turned back the page, reading the words written long ago in purple ink, now faded:

71

. . . Oh, why did I have to be the homely one?
Father loves Kathleen so much. They do everything
for *her*. Now this wonderful birthday party. And I
have to address all those invitations. The people in
town despise our family because we're northerners.
But they love Kathleen. They'll come to her party.

Meg suddenly felt terribly sorry for Amelia. She
was the homely daughter, hurt because she had to
help with the party for her beautiful, popular sister.
Still, she must have loved her very much to have kept
her room like that. Had she grieved all those years?

Meg jumped at a sound from the hall. Footsteps.
She dropped the notebook back into the drawer and
closed the desk lid. The footsteps were heavy, like
a man's. Impulsively Meg darted behind one of the
dusty draperies.

She heard the man come into the room, and she
took a cautious peek. A stranger—a youngish man
with a dark beard—stood looking around in a
puzzled way. Then he behaved very oddly. He
looked into the closet. He opened the cabinets. Then
he went through the contents of an old dresser that
stood in a corner.

Meg didn't know whether to speak or not. Who was he? she wondered.

In a moment, he turned and strode from the room. A bit later, Meg followed him down the stairs.

When she reached the lower hall, she heard voices in the drawing room. She went in. Uncle Hal was gone; he was taking pictures in the dining room. But Kathleen and her mother were there, with Kerry beside them. They all sat on the gilded chairs.

With them was the bearded young man.

Meg laughed to herself. He was the lawyer, of course. He must have come to the old house early and had been looking around on the third floor.

Kerry jumped up. She was a little bit angry with her friend for staying behind. "I was just about to come and get you," she said.

"This is Meg Duncan, Mr. Carberry," said Kathleen. "She knew my Aunt Amelia."

The lawyer nodded at Meg. He was taking an important-looking paper out of his briefcase.

Meg motioned to Kerry to come with her. "We'll wait out in the hall," she said politely.

Kathleen wouldn't hear of it. "He's going to tell us about the will," she said. "I want you to stay."

73

8
A STRANGE REQUEST

The stiff paper crackled in Mr. Carberry's hands as he unfolded it. "I'm not going to read all this legal matter," he said. "It will be easier just to tell you about your aunt's wishes."

He was looking directly at Kathleen. Meg saw that she sat stiffly, holding her hands rigidly in her lap.

The lawyer cleared his throat. "You might think that your aunt was a little crazy, Kathleen," he said, "but, believe me, she was as sane as you are. Amelia Hannigan had good reasons for everything she did. She wanted you to inherit this house—but she laid down certain conditions."

"Please go on, Mr. Carberry," said Kathleen's mother. "What does my daughter have to do?"

"First—the will asks Kathleen to live in this house for at least one month."

"Oh, no!" Kathleen looked at him beseechingly.

"Next—she is to be friendly with her neighbors in Hidden Springs. And at the end of the month, she is to give a party—a party for a hundred guests."

"A hundred guests!" Mrs. Martin looked bewildered. "I'm afraid that would be very expensive," she protested. "And I'm not sure it would be proper to invite people we hardly know to a party."

"Don't worry about the expense," replied the lawyer. "Money has been set aside to cover everything."

"And we can introduce you to people in town," Meg spoke up eagerly. "Kerry and I know lots of people. They'll just love Kathleen."

"And I'll bet they'll all want to come to that party," said Kerry, completely dazzled. "Everybody wants to see the inside of this old house. They'll really be surprised." She looked up at the glittering chandelier.

"I leave all that to you folks," said the lawyer.

"What if I don't live in the house and don't give the party?" asked Kathleen hesitantly.

"You just have to!" cried Meg. It was the most

exciting idea she had ever heard of.

"In that case," the lawyer answered Kathleen, "the property will go to another heir."

"Who?" asked Mrs. Martin.

"I can't tell you that. If Kathleen follows through with her aunt's plan, we will never tell the other heir. I strongly advise her to do it. This is a valuable legacy, Mrs. Martin."

"We'll have to go back to California in a few weeks," remarked Mrs. Martin. "I'm a schoolteacher, you know."

"After the party is over, Kathleen can do anything she wishes with the house," the lawyer said. "She may want to sell it. There is just one hitch," he added, looking serious. "I hate to tell you about it, but Miss Amelia wrote down exact instructions for the party, including the guest list. The problem is—we can't find them."

"What happened to them?" asked Kathleen. She was still looking dazed.

"I have no idea. Miss Amelia sent for me a few months ago, to make a new will. She told me she would mail me those papers. But she died rather suddenly, and I never received them."

Everyone stared anxiously at him. Without the

list and the plans for the party, Kathleen couldn't fulfill her aunt's request.

"Where do you suppose she put them?" she asked, looking helplessly around the big room. "How will we ever find them?"

"I don't know," said Mr. Carberry quietly. "But we'd better start looking. I came early today to look around but found nothing. You were given just four months to fulfill the terms of the will. Three are already gone. As you know, we lost valuable time trying to find you."

He glanced then at Meg and Kerry. "Perhaps these young ladies will help us search."

"Oh, will you?" begged Kathleen, turning to Meg and Kerry.

Both girls were on their feet at the same time. "Let's begin right now," said Meg.

So began the search for the missing guest list and Miss Amelia's instructions for the party. Everyone helped in the search. They looked in the old desks, in the closets and attics—even in little Kathleen's room.

There were many old papers and pictures, but there was no sign of the papers they sought.

In Miss Amelia's room, Meg looked through one

of the window seats while Uncle Hal went through the old rolltop desk and Kerry searched the closet. Meg was just about to start on the next window seat —the lid seemed to be stuck—when Kerry, emerging from the closet, had an idea.

"How about asking Miss Amelia's old housekeeper, Jenny Grayham? She might know where that paper is."

Meg didn't know Mrs. Grayham well, though she had seen her several times in the village. The woman used to do errands for Miss Amelia when the old lady was afraid to go out. "I think Constable Hosey knows where she moved to," she said thoughtfully.

Uncle Hal went to the nearest phone and called the constable. Mrs. Grayham lived just a short distance from the big house. Uncle Hal took the two younger girls to interview the woman.

Jenny Grayham was a thin, gray little woman, almost as shy as her employer had been.

"No." She shook her head when they questioned her. "I never saw any paper like that, but it's probably around there. Miss Amelia was always writing things down. I never asked questions."

Meg had a question, and she couldn't keep from asking it. "Why did Miss Amelia keep some of the rooms so beautiful and let the rest of the house stay so shabby?''

''I don't know,'' the little woman answered with a frown. ''She must have loved that dead sister of hers. She was always talking about her, telling me how sweet she was. . . . She kept me so busy keeping her room spic-and-span and shining up the silver, I didn't have time to clean all the house. And she'd never let me put a foot in that room of hers.

''She wasn't crazy, though,'' she added loyally as her visitors started for the door. ''She had her own way of doing things, but she was real generous. She paid the way for my boy, Harley, to go to school. He has a fine job with the phone company over in Big Fork. . . . There he is now,'' she added.

A small green car was coming up the drive, a young man at the wheel. He appeared to be about in his mid-twenties. He glared at the group on the porch. As Uncle Hal started to speak to him, he jumped out of the car. He brushed right past them and went into the house.

Meg wondered indignantly what he had learned in college. He certainly hadn't learned good manners.

When they returned to the Hannigan house, the lost papers had just been found—by Kathleen herself.

They were in a perfectly obvious place—inside Amelia's shabby old purse, hanging in the closet. They were in an envelope, addressed to the lawyer and already stamped for mailing.

Kathleen came running triumphantly down the stairs. She handed the envelope to Mr. Carberry.

"She must have meant to send them and then got sick," he remarked. He opened the envelope and glanced at the contents. Then he handed the papers to Mrs. Martin. "I'm glad we found them."

Meg and Kerry were hoping that Mrs. Martin would look at the papers. They were curious to know about that party. But she put the envelope in her own purse.

"You've had enough excitement for one day, Kathleen," she said. "We'll read this tonight at the motel." Then she sighed wearily. "I suppose we'll have to move into this old place tomorrow," she said.

"Poor Kathleen," Meg said softly, when she and Kerry were on their way home with Uncle Hal. "She really doesn't want to stay in that place."

"I don't blame her," said Kerry. "It's fun to go there in the daytime, but I wouldn't want to spend the night there."

"Especially if the noisy ghosts start banging on

the woodwork,'' said Uncle Hal in a spectral voice.

Meg grinned. ''Well, we didn't see or hear any ghosts today,'' she said. ''And we looked all over the house. Maybe Mrs. Martin is right, and Kathleen just imagines she hears things.''

''We'll find out for sure—after tomorrow,'' said Kerry ominously.

9
A MYSTERIOUS ACCIDENT

It wasn't much trouble for Kathleen Martin and her mother to move to the Hannigan house. They had only their car and suitcases and a tiny white poodle named Cherie. But Mrs. Martin insisted upon tidying the place up before she would live there.

She hired Jenny Grayham to come and stay in her old room and help with the cleaning. And she enlisted the help of Meg and Kerry and the Carmody twins. They carried box after box of junk into the attic and basement.

The boys were shy about going into the cellar, but Meg laughed at them and dared them to go with her. She wanted to see the inside of that wine room herself.

It was just as they had said. There was an old wine

rack with a few dusty bottles and a workbench covered with wire and odd gadgets. The door lock was still broken.

Meg examined it carefully. The door was heavy and creaky. It must have swung shut of its own weight, locking the boys in. Meg discovered one other thing that wasn't easy to explain.

On the floor near the workbench was a fresh apple core. Somebody must have dropped it there. She couldn't quite picture in her mind a ghost eating an apple!

There were lights in the house now, and a telephone had been installed. When the man from the power company came, he had discovered an odd thing. A wire had been strung from the light poles directly to the house. The electricity had been on all the time. But all the bulbs in the house had been screwed loose!

"Why would anybody do that?" Mrs. Martin had asked.

For a while, everything was peaceful at the mansion. Kathleen helped her mother fix a big room for them to sleep in. Meg and Kerry introduced the girl to their friends in Hidden Springs.

Mrs. Partlow was especially delighted with Kathleen. And after she invited the Martins to her home for tea, other neighbors did likewise.

Kathleen even had a date with Kerry's older brother, Bill, who was just her age. They went to a movie and afterward to the drugstore for ice cream.

Kerry was angry because Bill wouldn't let her and Meg tag along. Meg just laughed.

"Kathleen is old enough to have dates," she said tolerantly. "And pretty enough, too. I don't blame Bill for wanting to be alone with her."

The town buzzed with gossip about Amelia Hannigan's strange will—and about the big party. Why was it being put on, and who was to be invited? Even Meg and Kerry didn't know. Meanwhile, Kathleen and her mother kept their secrets and went ahead with elaborate plans for the fantastic affair.

Then all at once the peace was shattered. The noisy ghost came back.

The girls had ridden out to the Hannigan house with a loaf of Mrs. Wilson's freshly baked bread. As they stood in the front hall, Kathleen came racing down from upstairs, almost hysterical. She had heard the ghostly footsteps again. Her eyes were wild.

"Mother doesn't believe me," she cried, "but she's

never there when it happens. It's somebody run-ning—running—right behind me. And nobody is ever there!''

Meg put a firm hand on the girl's arm. ''Please don't be frightened, Kathleen,'' she begged. ''There must be some explanation. Kerry and I will go back with you. We'll see if it happens again.''

Kathleen went reluctantly back up the steps, Meg and Kerry in front of her. They walked all the way to the end of the hall. Then they turned and came back down the steps.

Nothing happened.

Meg was baffled. She knew Kathleen wasn't making this up. Why couldn't others hear the foot-steps?

''It seems almost as if something is trying to force me out of this house,'' said Kathleen. ''Maybe Aunt Amelia didn't love me, after all. Maybe she just brought me here so she could h-h-haunt me.''

Later that same day, something else happened—this time to Meg herself. She heard Cherie barking in the drawing room. She walked in and looked around.

There was an old-fashioned piano in the corner, and the tiny white dog was jumping against it. Meg stared at it as she sat down on one of the small chairs.

Suddenly the piano began to play—all by itself.

For a moment, Meg was too stunned to move. Then she got up and walked toward it. She opened the front panel and found that it was a player piano. The disk was turning with the paper record, and the pedals were moving up and down, as if pumped by ghostly feet.

Meg picked up the poodle and petted her. She looked behind the piano but could see no wires.

The music stopped as abruptly as it had begun, and Meg ran from the room.

The others had been in the kitchen. They hurried into the hall.

"I thought I heard music," Mrs. Martin said. "Were you playing the piano, Meg?"

Meg managed to smile. But she didn't tell what had happened—not just then. Kathleen was upset enough.

Still shaken, Meg told Kerry about it on the way home.

Kerry looked at her with gloomy eyes. "I was beginning to think Kathleen was just cuckoo," she said. "Now you're hearing things, too. This is the goofiest mystery yet, Meg. We helped catch that jewel thief, and we found the lost silver for the Ashley sisters. But how can you trap something you can't even *see* or *feel?*"

That night, Meg wrote a long letter to her father. He was still away in Europe on some secret government business. She always missed him terribly when he was away.

I know you don't believe in ghosts, Daddy, she wrote, *but I just don't know what to think. It would be sad if the Martins were scared into leaving that old house.*

She was drifting off to sleep when the telephone rang. It rang and rang, almost as if it were frantic. Her heart thudding, Meg got out of bed and ran out to the landing. She hung over the banister to listen.

Mrs. Wilson, in curlers and robe, was on the phone. "Yes, yes," she said excitedly. "My, oh, my, how dreadful!"

She turned to look up at Meg.

Meg knew even before she spoke that it must be Kathleen. "What happened?" she asked.

"There has been an accident at the big house. Mrs. Martin went to let the dog out the back door.

There was a loose step, and she fell. . . ."

Meg raced down the steps and took the phone. "Kathleen?" she said.

"Oh, Meg!" The girl seemed ready to cry.

"Was your mother hurt much?"

"No. She just scraped her leg. But I know that step wasn't loose this afternoon. And I'm the one who usually lets the dog out—"

That accident was meant to happen to *Kathleen.*

"I really called to ask about a doctor. Mother should be checked, to be sure no bones are broken. If he says it's all right, we're going right back to the motel. I won't stay in this dreadful place another night."

"But you can't!" wailed Meg. "You have to stay a month. Remember? You don't want to lose the house."

She looked up Dr. Evans's number and gave it to Kathleen. Then she said, "Hold on a minute, Kathleen."

Meg turned to Mrs. Wilson. She was careful to say nothing about that loose step. "She's terribly worried, Mrs. Wilson. Do you suppose Mr. Wilson would drive me over there right now?"

Mrs. Wilson shook her head. "I can't allow you

to do that, Meg, in the middle of the night. What would your father say? Those old run-down houses are dangerous.''

''Daddy would say, 'Let her go,' '' declared Meg confidently. ''He would want me to help. And Kathleen needs me. What could happen?'' she demanded. ''The housekeeper is there—and Mrs. Martin, too. I can sleep with Kathleen.''

Even Mrs. Wilson was quite helpless when Meg became quiet and logical like that. In the end, she got her husband out of bed. He dressed reluctantly and drove Meg to the old house.

''Now, you call me right away if you need me,'' he ordered as he left her at the door.

The grateful Kathleen was waiting in the hall. She threw her arms around her young visitor.

''Oh, Meg, you're an angel,'' she cried. ''I wouldn't have stayed if you hadn't come.''

As they started up the stairway, a door near the end of the hall opened a crack, and a small old face peered out curiously. Meg felt a shiver go through her.

It was only the housekeeper, Jenny Grayham, but even that little old lady looked suspicious on a night like this.

91

10
A CABLE FOR MEG

Mrs. Martin was not badly hurt. The doctor came and went. He advised bed rest for a day or two.

She had lost some of her spirit, however. She was alarmed by what had happened.

"I was all wrong about Kathleen," she said when Meg came into her bedroom. "She wasn't imagining things, after all. That step on the porch was deliberately loosened by somebody—or something."

Meg made up her mind to look at the step first thing in the morning. "It could be just rotted out, like a lot of things around here," she said brightly. "When Kathleen inherits this land, she can sell a piece of it and restore the place. People say it was very beautiful in the old days."

"*If* Kathleen inherits the house," Mrs. Martin said.

"We still have two weeks to go before we give that party. I'm not sure we can stand it that long."

She sighed deeply. "It seemed like a miracle when we first heard of Aunt Amelia's will. Kathleen's father died when she was a baby. I could never do much for her. With this legacy, she could go to college and—"

"Go to sleep now, Mother, and don't think about it." Kathleen bent and kissed her mother's cheek. "Come on, Meg," she added. "You'll have to sleep with me in the other bed—unless you want one of those spooky old rooms."

Meg shook her head firmly. She had brought a small overnight bag. She quickly changed back into her pajamas and crawled into bed beside Kathleen. The poodle jumped onto the coverlet and snuggled near her feet.

With Meg there, Kathleen went to sleep almost instantly. Meg lay awake, listening to the sounds of the old house.

In the middle of the night, she thought she heard the back door open and close. It always squeaked. She slipped silently out of bed and into the hall. From a rear window, she looked out on the back garden. She was startled to see a small, shadowy figure just disappearing among the trees.

She was almost sure it was old Jenny Grayham, the housekeeper. What was she doing out there at this time of the night? Then Meg remembered that Mrs. Grayham lived somewhere beyond the Hannigan property.

Still puzzled, Meg crept back into bed. The house was quiet for the rest of the night. In the morning, Mrs. Grayham was in the kitchen, silent and mousy, as usual. She fixed breakfast for the girls, and they ate on trays in the room with Mrs. Martin.

As soon as she could, Meg slipped outside and examined the loose step on the back porch. There were clean scratches. The nails had been pulled recently, and the board tipped forward at a touch.

Meg stood up and looked around. What menace, she asked herself, hung over this house? Who had slipped up, unseen, to cause such mischief?

Later that morning, Meg called Mrs. Wilson and told her she was safe and sound. She asked if she might stay till afternoon. Then she called Kerry and reported the events of the night.

Kerry was quite envious.

"You said you wouldn't stay in the haunted house," Meg reminded her.

"I wouldn't mind, as long as you were there."

"My fan!" said Meg. "I'm going to stay every night if Mrs. Wilson will let me. We just *have* to help the Martins solve this mystery, Kerry—before something terrible happens."

"I'm tired of hearing about spooks," said Kerry plaintively. "Let's go horseback riding this afternoon, Meg." The Carmodys owned several saddle horses.

Mr. Wilson came for Meg about two-thirty. After she mailed her letter to her father, she and Kerry went for a ride along the river.

That evening, Mrs. Carmody invited her to stay for dinner. Meg enjoyed southern-fried chicken and strawberry shortcake, but there was no vacation from spooks. All anybody could talk about was the haunted house.

Meg stayed with Kathleen that night. The very next day she heard those ghostly footsteps herself. Kerry, who was visiting, heard them, too.

Kathleen had called them from the head of the stairs, and they both went running up the carpeted steps. Kerry put a hand on the banister. Just then the noise began.

Meg stopped short. Kerry looked at her, her

freckled face pale. It sounded like somebody running in front of them down the hall—somebody in a desperate hurry. No one was there but Kathleen, and she wasn't moving.

"You see, I *did* hear it!" she cried. She didn't seem so frightened now, however, with them there. "What is it, Meg?"

The sound had stopped by now. Meg ran her fingers along the railing. She walked slowly down the hall, then bent and pushed aside the long faded runner. The floor was old and worn, but there was no sign of tampering.

In the following days, the noisy ghost seemed to become more active than ever. The piano played all by itself. There were strange rappings in the walls. Another plate jumped from the plate rail.

The Martins were becoming more and more nervous, and it was becoming more difficult for them to stay in the house. Even Meg was afraid something worse might happen.

Finally Constable Hosey was called in. He looked at the loose porch step and carefully checked the piano. The noisy ghost was perfectly quiet while he was around.

He even questioned Jenny Grayham.

"Did these funny noises happen when Miss Amelia was alive?" he asked.

She was washing dishes, and she went right on, not looking at the constable. "Old houses always make funny noises," she said evasively.

The constable shook his head in disgust. "Can't catch a rascal unless you can *see* him," he said.

Newspapermen heard of the ghosts in the Hannigan house. They came from the city, pestering Kathleen and her mother with questions—questions that had no answers.

Then real estate people began to bother them. Two men were very obnoxious.

"We've had our eye on this place for a long time, miss," one of them told Kathleen. "As soon as you get title, we want to buy it."

"I don't even *own* it," said the distracted girl.

"Well, we won't give up. We want to tear down this old ruin and build a number of houses. If you don't inherit the place, we'll try to buy it from the other heir."

Kathleen closed the door—hard. A mirror fell from the wall and broke. The girl was almost frantic.

Then, somehow—adding to the mystery—the

little white poodle got trapped in the cellar. Meg and Kathleen could hear him barking and whining from below the floor.

"Now what?" cried Kathleen. She and Meg ran together to the inside cellar door.

To their amazement, they found Mrs. Grayham already in the cellar. She had a dish of ground meat in her hand. She was trying to coax the little dog to eat it.

Kathleen flew down the steps and grabbed the dish of meat. Meg gathered up the tiny dog. When they went back to the kitchen, Kathleen threw the meat into the garbage.

"It's probably poisoned!" she sobbed.

"Why, what do you mean?" Jenny Grayham had followed them back up the stairs, and she came into the kitchen, looking hurt.

"I wouldn't poison your little dog," she said. "Somebody closed him in the cellar. He wouldn't come to me, so I was just trying to coax him back upstairs."

Meg felt as if her head were spinning round and round. She was just as confused as everybody else. She was almost ready to give up.

Then the cablegram came from her father.

11
THE THINKING CAP

Mr. Wilson drove out to the Hannigan house to bring Meg home. He gave her the cablegram in the car.

"Mrs. Wilson was afraid it might be important," he said.

Anxiously Meg opened the envelope and read the message. She stared at the yellow paper for a long time. Then she began to laugh.

"Glad it isn't bad news, Miss Meg," said Mr. Wilson.

The message read:

PUT ON YOUR THINKING CAP, MARGARET. GHOSTLY SHENANIGANS ARE USUALLY THE WORK OF HUMAN HANDS.   DAD.

"What does it mean?" asked Kerry when Meg showed it to her later in Meg's big, airy room.

"Exactly what it says, Kerry," said Meg. "It means that somebody pretty smart has been up to tricks, and we'd better get smart, too, if we're going to catch him in time. Kerry," she ordered, "bring me the dictionary."

Kerry jumped up and found the dictionary on Meg's bookshelf.

"Poltergeist," said Meg, flipping the pages. "Here it is: 'A noisy ghost; a ghost supposedly responsible for table tappings and other mysterious noises.'"

"We knew that already," said Kerry.

"Now bring me a pencil and paper, please," said Meg.

Flat on her stomach, she drew a line down the middle of the paper and began to make two lists:

GHOSTLY TRICKS	OTHER PUZZLES
1. Running footsteps	1. Cellar doors
2. The piano playing	2. Broken stairstep
3. Wall tappings	3. Apple core
4. Falling plates	4. Light bulbs twisted
5. Phantom figures	5. Dog in cellar

Kerry stared at the lists doubtfully. "I can't see how that will help us solve the mystery," she said.

"Can't you?" Meg sat up. "There *might* be some ghosts around that house. Even Uncle Hal isn't sure about ghosts. I suppose a poltergeist could play those noisy tricks. But a ghost didn't close those cellar doors while you and I were gone to get help for the twins.

"And a ghost didn't take the nails out of that step so somebody would fall," Meg went on. "Would a ghost unscrew the light bulbs—or eat an apple in the old wine room?"

Kerry was nodding her blond head. "You're right, Meg. But that doesn't tell us what the twins saw near the summerhouse."

"No," Meg admitted. "But we don't have to worry about *her*. She isn't harming anybody. But something—or somebody—is. And I *don't* believe it's another ghost," Meg added grimly.

"I think those tricks are being done by human hands—just as Daddy says. And we'd better get busy and find out whose hands they are—before Kathleen gets scared away and loses her inheritance."

"Or before somebody gets hurt again," said Kerry gravely. "But, Meg, if somebody *is* sneaking around that house, why can't we see him?"

"I don't know," said Meg. "There are lots of

rooms and lots of places to hide. The Martins hardly ever go on the third floor. Yesterday, when I was up there, I had a feeling somebody was watching."

"Brrrrr!" Kerry rolled her eyes.

"And sometimes Kathleen's little dog sets up a fuss, for no reason we can see. Dogs can hear things human beings can't, you know."

Just then Meg's cat—a beautiful Siamese named Thunder—jumped from the bed. Kerry tried to pet him, but he wouldn't let her. Instead he curled up in Meg's lap.

Meg patted him lovingly. "Whoever is trying to drive the Martins from that house is as clever as a cat," she declared. "You never hear him, except when he wants you to. I wonder who it can be."

Meg put on her thinking cap as her father had suggested. She looked off into space. Suddenly she pushed Thunder from her lap. She grabbed the paper again and turned it over.

"Let's make a list of suspects," she said. "It could be one of those real estate men. They want that property awfully bad. Maybe they think if they can scare Kathleen away, they can buy it from the other heir!"

She wrote something on the paper.

Kerry was frowning. "It might even be one of the neighbors, somebody who doesn't want the Martins to live in Hidden Springs. . . . It might even be Mrs. Partlow's daughter-in-law, Elizabeth. She always wanted that house, and she looks down her nose at everybody."

Meg laughed. "Mrs. Partlow would wring her neck. She's become very fond of Kathleen."

She touched the tip of her pencil to her tongue.

"Constable Hosey thinks it might be a tramp," she said thoughtfully. "And the twins think it might be a foreign spy—using the house to send messages. It could even be that other heir," she said suddenly, "the one who will get the house if Kathleen doesn't give the party."

"That person doesn't even know about the will," Kerry reminded her. "The lawyer isn't going to tell him till later."

"That's so." But Meg wrote it down, anyway. "The most suspicious one so far," she added, "is old Jenny Grayham. She's acted awfully funny lately."

"That little old lady wouldn't be able to climb a light pole," Kerry retorted. "Don't forget, somebody had wired the electricity directly to the house."

Electricity. The word was like a switch, turning on a light in Meg's brain. Suddenly she put down her pencil and sprang to her feet. "That gives me an idea, Kerry. Let's go out and see Kathleen right now."

Kerry ran to get her bike.

Mrs. Martin and her daughter were polishing silver trays when the two girls arrived. They both looked nervous and pale.

"Kerry and I think all this ghost stuff is trickery," said Meg. "Somebody is just trying to make you think the house is haunted."

"It's scary, just the same," said Kathleen. "Mother might have been killed on that step."

"That's why we have to find out who's doing these tricks. And why. And how. Kerry and I have been thinking."

"Excuse me a minute, girls," Mrs. Martin said. "We seem to be running out of polish."

Meg showed Kathleen the two lists. "Remember all those wires and tools and things in the basement, Kathleen?"

Kathleen nodded, her eyes puzzled.

"Remember how the bulbs were all screwed out —so whoever came in would think the electricity was off? . . . You heard those ghostly footsteps that first day. I think those noises were made by magic, instead of ghosts."

"Magic?"

"Modern magic," said Meg firmly. "With electricity, maybe. Come on. Let's go make that ghost walk again." Meg felt quite calm.

Kathleen and Kerry followed her into the hall. "You always heard the footsteps when you were near the top of the stairs," she said to Kathleen. "Now you and Kerry run up and down till it happens again."

Meg stood at the bottom of the stairwell while her two friends pranced up and down the stairs. She saw that Kerry usually went up the middle of the steps. The older girl walked close to the banister.

"There it goes, Meg!" Kathleen halted on the top step.

As Meg raced up to join them, she heard the sound of running footsteps.

Meg wasn't the least bit awed by it this time. She got down on her hands and knees and felt along the ends of the last two steps. She found a slight bump under the faded carpeting.

The carpet was tacked down, but it was weak from age. Excitedly Meg tore it back with her fingers.

There was a small button on the surface of the step. By now the ghostly sound had faded. She pressed the button with her finger and heard the sound again.

An electronic ghost was running along the hallway.

12
IN THE CELLAR

Meg had Kerry press the small button, while she walked slowly along the hall. Near the middle of the floor, she could *feel* the sound. It vibrated through the old boards.

"Let's see what's below this," said Meg. She led the way downstairs. Standing in the center of the downstairs hall, she looked up. A heavy crystal chandelier hung down. Against the ceiling was a brass plate.

Meg pointed up. "There's your running ghost, Kathleen," she said. "It's under the floorboards of the upstairs hall—wired from that chandelier. It may be an electric clapper, or even a tape recording of somebody's footsteps. It's wired to that button on the stairs."

Kathleen stared admiringly at Meg.

"Now for that piano that plays all by itself," said Meg. She took them into the drawing room. "I was right over here," she said. "I sat down in this chair."

She sat. There was a whirring sound. Instantly the piano began to play. Meg examined the chair. There were no gadgets. But when she moved to one side, the music started up again.

Her eyes gleamed. "That's it," she said. "The switch must be worked by a ray—an electric eye, like they use to open and close doors. There's wiring in the piano that makes the pedals work—"

"Like the door in the cellar!" cried Kerry. "Remember? The twins said it opened like the door in the supermarket. And it closed by itself. Nobody had to lock them in!"

"That's right," said Meg. "There's a rubber mat in front of it. There could be a switch under that. Then Constable Hosey broke the lock, so it quit working."

Kathleen's pretty face was hopeful now.

"Whoever did this knows all about electronics," said Meg. "This old place is rigged like a spook house."

"It certainly is," said Kathleen. "I've been scared

out of my wits ever since I came here. The question is: Who's doing these tricks?''

Even Meg couldn't answer that. But before she could say anything, something else happened. There was a faint chiming sound from the mantel, and the three girls turned to look. On the mantel stood two gilt candlesticks. Glass prisms hung from them. The noisy ghost was busy again. The crystals were swaying against each other, making a soft, eerie tinkling sound.

Meg walked slowly to the fireplace. There was a little frown on her forehead. Reaching high to touch the wooden mantel, she felt a faint vibration under her fingers.

"The fireplace wall goes down into the cellar," she murmured. "The twins said there was a dumb-waiter next to it."

At one end of the fireplace, she found a small door in the paneling. She opened it carefully and peered down into the dark recess.

"The boys heard footsteps through that," Kerry whispered. "They might have heard Kathleen, when she was in this room—"

"Shhh!" Meg's lips barely moved on the word. She was listening. She heard a shoving sound from

below—as if something heavy were being forced into the dumbwaiter box. The movement was jarring the wooden panel. That's what made the glass prisms chime!

Pulling Kerry along with her, Meg walked over to Kathleen. "I think our ghost is in the cellar right now," she said in a low voice. Her eyes were bright. "Maybe we can catch him if we hurry. Are you two game to go with me?"

They simply nodded.

The kitchen was quite dark. Meg cautiously opened the cellar door and started down. She didn't dare switch on the lights. Her heart was thumping so hard it hurt.

"Don't make a sound," she warned in a whisper.

They were too late. Meg had gone only a couple of steps when she saw that the outside cellar doors were open. A pair of legs was visible for an instant through the opening.

The wide doors came slowly together.

Their "ghost" had escaped, but not before Meg had seen something: The "ghost" was wearing men's shoes.

"I'm sure he didn't see us," said Meg. The three hurried back into the kitchen, then out the kitchen door. "Watch out for that loose step," warned Meg, jumping over it.

There was no sign of the intruder. Whoever it was had vanished among the trees. A moment later, they heard the sound of a car starting up beyond the fence. It roared away.

"Maybe he just comes here once in a while," said Meg thoughtfully. "Maybe on weekends or at night. He doesn't have to get into the house often because those noisy gadgets seem to be automatic."

"He must have sneaked in today," said Kerry positively, "because that piano played a different piece today."

"He could have sneaked up through the kitchen when nobody was watching," suggested Kathleen.

Meg's eyes grew narrow. "I'm almost sure he was trying to hide something in that dumbwaiter. Let's go take a look."

Mrs. Martin, holding a fresh jar of silver polish, met them in the kitchen. When she heard what had happened, she refused to let the girls go into the cellar.

"Would you please call your friend Constable Hosey, Meg?" she asked.

When Constable Hosey arrived, the girls showed

him the button under the carpet that turned on the ghostly footsteps. Meg sat on the chair and made the old-fashioned piano play all by itself.

Hosey himself solved the riddle of the "jumping" plates. He felt under the shelf and found a tiny windup mechanism. He pulled it loose and showed it to them.

"It's got a timer on it," he said. "Just like an oven timer. It's set to go off now and then. It starts shaking that shelf and makes those plates jump off."

He looked at Meg and Kerry with grudging admiration. "You two have uncovered a devilish plan for sure, this time," he said. "We'd better take another look in that cellar to see if we can find out what this character is up to."

Kathleen was able to laugh now at the ghostly noises in the old house. But she couldn't laugh about what Constable Hosey found in the wine cellar.

Meg led him first to the dumbwaiter, near the fireplace wall. Just as she had suspected, their "ghost" had stuffed something into it—a gunnysack filled with bumpy items.

Constable Hosey emptied it out onto the workbench. There was a small tape recorder and a radio receiver, among other curious things. The constable picked up a buttonlike object and held it under the light.

"Do you know what that is, Meg?" he asked.

Meg shook her dark braids.

"That's a 'bug'—a listening device. The kind the spies use to listen in on government secrets."

But the most alarming discovery was hidden under the bench. It was a can of chloroform.

Meg shivered when she learned what it was.

"That was probably intended for Kathleen's little dog," Hosey said, his voice harsh. "She was probably getting to be too much of a problem for our tricky visitor."

Kathleen gave a horrified gasp. "When I get hold of her, I'll keep her with me every minute," she declared. "It's only a few days more till we have to mail the invitations for the party," she added, "but I don't see how we can stay here now. What if he comes back?"

"That's just what we want him to do," said Meg flatly. "He may not know yet that we're onto his tricks. We can keep a watch out for him all the time. If he comes back to use that chloroform, we can trap him."

115

13
THE HOWLING GHOST

"An excellent idea, Meg," said Constable Hosey, when he had heard Meg's plan for trapping the "ghost." "This is Saturday. If this rascal does his prowling nights and weekends, he might try to pull his big act today—or tonight."

"There's an old carriage shed in the side yard," the constable added. "I'll sneak a deputy in there. He can keep an eye on the outside cellar doors."

Constable Hosey advised Mrs. Martin to keep the door leading from the kitchen to the basement locked.

"At all times," he said. "We know he has a key to the padlock outside. He can get in there, but we won't let him get out. The basement windows are too small for a man to go through. If we play our

116

cards right, we have a good chance of landing this spook.''

Kathleen had begun searching for her dog.

"Cherie! Cherie!''

Meg, hearing her calling the little poodle, had a sudden fearful thought. Had some of that chloroform already been used?

They all began a frantic search for the small dog. They looked inside the house and out. Then, to their relief, when they were in the big downstairs hall, they heard a small yip. The sound came from Jenny Grayham's room!

Kathleen rapped loudly on the door. When the housekeeper opened it, she had the tiny poodle in her arms. Mrs. Grayham was smiling uncertainly.

"She finally made friends with me,'' the old lady said, sounding pleased. "I gave her a bone, and she came right to me.'' She petted the dog's snowy fur.

"Oh, thank goodness!'' Kathleen grabbed Cherie and held her. "We—we were afraid she was lost.''

"That old lady acts awfully odd sometimes,'' said Kerry, after the door had closed and Mrs. Grayham had gone.

"I know it,'' said Kathleen. "Mother would like to let her go, but we need her. She knows where everything is in this old house. And you have no idea of all we have to do for that party.''

The plan to trap the strange prankster had seemed like a good one when Meg thought of it. But as she lay in bed that night, she thought of a flaw. What if whoever was behind all this got into the house through a window? What if he meant that chloroform for Kathleen and not the dog?

Meg punched Kathleen gently in the ribs.

''Let's go downstairs and keep an eye on that cellar door,'' she whispered. ''We can hide in the pantry.''

The pantry was opposite the door. They took a blanket and slipped downstairs. They left the pantry door open a crack.

As Meg huddled against the wall, she felt a little guilty. She had warned Kerry, when she went home, not to mention the alarming events at the big house. And she had told the Wilsons nothing. She didn't want to worry them. She could take care of herself, she had thought. Now she wasn't so sure.

Nothing happened for some time. Both girls dozed off. Then Meg awoke with a start as the pantry door suddenly snapped shut. Kathleen slept on.

Meg jumped to her feet and pushed against it. The old-fashioned latch on the outside was locked!

Meg heard someone open the cellar door. She thought fast. They had made a plan to signal the deputy if anything happened inside the house. They were to turn on the upstairs lights and scream. They couldn't do that now.

Meg pulled the light chain. "Wake up, Kathleen!" she shouted. Then she grabbed the first thing she saw—a heavy canister of flour. She pitched it with all her might through the pantry window.

She began to shout at the top of her voice. "Help! Help! We need you!"

Kathleen didn't know what it was all about, but she started to scream, too.

It was only a moment before the deputy came running in from the carriage house. He unlatched the pantry door.

He was a huge young man. "What's up, Miss Meg?" he said breathlessly. "I didn't see a thing."

"The cellar!" cried Meg.

The door was standing open. They all ran to it. The young officer led the way down the stairs.

And now, for the first time, they heard the "ghost" himself. He was howling at the top of his lungs. "Let me out of here! Let me out of here!"

Meg had switched on the cellar light. Now she and Kathleen stopped dead still in the middle of the stairs. They looked down upon one of the strangest sights they had ever seen.

Jenny Grayham, in nightgown and robe, was sitting on top of a huge trunk. Somehow she had shoved the heavy object against the wine cellar door.

The "ghost" was behind that door, slowly pushing it outward. "What are you doing, for pete's sake?" he shouted.

Meg could barely see his furious face. For a moment, she had no idea who he was. Then the truth struck her. It was the woman's own son, Harley Grayham!

"Get away from there, Ma! Let me out," he wailed.

"I'll move," the old lady said, "when I learn what you're up to, boy. I've had a feeling it was you doing those awful tricks."

By then the deputy was there. He helped Mrs. Grayham down from the trunk. Then he pulled it aside and hauled forth the angry young man.

Grabbing him by the arm, he led him up the steps, into the kitchen. The excited girls scampered before him. And Jenny Grayham, with as much dignity as possible, followed.

The deputy shoved Harley Grayham into a kitchen chair.

"All right, young fellow," he said. "You've got some explaining to do. You've had these poor folks scared half to death. Do you want to talk now, or—"

Jenny Grayham wasn't that gentle. She strode purposefully up to her son, grasped him firmly by both shoulders, and shook him soundly.

"Yes, boy. What do you mean by trying to scare Miss Kathleen from this house? Speak up!"

Harley looked back sullenly.

"I did it," he admitted finally. "But it was for you, Ma. I didn't want to hurt anybody. I just wanted to make them get out of this house. It rightfully belongs to us. Do you know who was going to get it if they didn't?"

"No, I don't, and I don't care," said the small woman stoutly. "You did wrong, Harley Grayham!"

"It really belongs to us," the young man whined. "Miss Hannigan left it to you in her will. Those people don't have any right to it."

He pointed a shaking finger at Kathleen and her mother. Mrs. Martin had heard the noise and was now downstairs. In her arms was the small poodle.

"You're the one who took care of that old lady all those years, Ma. And she paid you almost nothing," he said bitterly.

"That ain't so, Harley, and you know it. Miss Amelia paid me enough. And she was good to you, too—letting you live here with me when you were little. Don't forget, it was Miss Amelia sent you to electronics school and let you have that shop in the basement."

Meg was getting impatient, and she was full of questions, as usual. "Was your mother the other heir the lawyer spoke about?" she asked. "Was she supposed to get this house if Kathleen didn't?"

The boy nodded. "It belongs to us."

"But how did you know about the will?" Meg asked curiously. "The lawyer didn't tell anybody."

The boy laughed. "That was the easiest part of all," he said. "Ma didn't know it, but I had the old lady's library bugged. I listened down in the cellar when she told the lawyer what to put in the will.

"I knew if I scared *her* away"—he pointed to Kathleen—"the house would be mine and Ma's. It was worth a try. She was almost ready to give up."

"Then Meg came along," said Mrs. Martin, putting her arm around the girl. "And, with that thinking cap of hers, solved the mystery. We know all about your poltergeist tricks, young man."

"Well, what are we waiting for?" Harley held out his hands to the deputy. "I suppose you're ready to put the handcuffs on me."

The big police officer shook his head. "That won't be necessary, boy," he said. "But I will have to call Constable Hosey out here. You'll have to talk to him. It's up to the Martins whether or not they want to press charges.

"One more question, though," he added. "How did you get into the cellar tonight? We had the doors locked, and I was watching the outside cellar doorway."

The boy managed a brazen grin. "There are a dozen ways to get into this old ruin," he retorted. "Tonight I came through the bathroom window near Ma's room."

"Yes, and I heard you sneaking in," said that old lady. "Took me a minute to get my robe and slippers, but—"

"Was it you who locked Meg and me in the pantry?" asked Kathleen.

For a moment, Jenny Grayham looked puzzled.

Then she nodded. "Guess I did. I didn't know you was in there, though. Miss Amelia always wanted that door kept closed. I guess I just pushed it shut on my way to the cellar."

The little old lady seemed to have shrunk even smaller. She looked more timid and mousy than ever—now that she had done what she had to do. Meg felt sorry for her.

Kathleen went over and put an arm around her. "I must apologize, Mrs. Grayham," she said. "I was almost ready to suspect *you.*"

"I'm afraid I suspected you, too," said Meg. "I did see you leave the house in the middle of the night."

Jenny Grayham smiled wanly. "Yes, I was feeling poorly that night. I forgot to bring my stomach medicine along. Mrs. Martin was hurt, and I didn't want to upset her. I went home to get my pills."

Even the deputy grinned as he went to telephone Constable Hosey.

14
A PARTY FOR KATHLEEN

After Constable Hosey had come and gone, taking the deflated "ghost" with him, the two girls and Mrs. Martin sat in the kitchen, talking. They felt too keyed up to go right to bed.

Kathleen was relieved that the intruder had been caught, but her ordeal was not yet over. She was very anxious about the coming party.

"The invitations came from the printer today," she told Meg. "I have to address them tomorrow. Oh, Meg, I'm so worried about it all. Aunt Amelia left such crazy instructions. I'm afraid it will be a dreadful flop."

Meg pressed her hand.

"How could it be, with you as hostess?" she said warmly. "I'm sure it will be a wonderful party."

She wasn't really sure, of course, even though exciting preparations had been going on around her for days. The florist had come to talk about flowers. Great boxes of fine foods had arrived. But so far Kathleen had kept most of her plans a secret from everyone, including Meg.

Meg wasn't even sure that *she* was going to be invited.

Two days later, the invitations began to arrive.

Meg, home again, heard a shout from beneath her window. It was Kerry. She was waving something square and white in her hand.

"It came, it came!" she cried. "Run and look in your mailbox, Meg. See if you got one, too."

Meg had been putting her books in order. Now she dropped everything and flew out the door. She was in such a hurry to get downstairs that she slid down the banister.

"Meg!" Mrs. Wilson, in the lower hall, was startled when the girl came swooping toward her. "You could hurt yourself."

Meg didn't hear her. She was soon outside, peering hopefully into the mailbox. Kerry came running around the corner of the house.

And there it was, with her father's mail—an invitation for Meg to the fantastic party to be held at the old Hannigan mansion.

It was to be a costume party. The guests on the list Miss Amelia had left were all invited. And a very select list that was.

Kerry and her mother and older brothers were invited—but her father was not. Meg's Uncle Hal got an invitation at his apartment in Washington—but Meg's own father was left out.

"And he'll be home next week, too," said Meg wistfully. "Not that Daddy would care."

"Don't feel bad." Kerry had heard her mother talking on the phone. "A lot of people are disappointed. Old Mrs. Partlow was asked, of course, but that snooty daughter-in-law of hers wasn't. I'll bet she's furious."

It became obvious that only people related to the old Hidden Springs families had been on the guest list.

"I didn't expect them to invite kids," said Kerry. "I wonder why they did. . . ."

Meg looked thoughtful. There were still mysteries about Amelia Hannigan to be solved. "I don't know," she said. "But Miss Amelia always seemed to like us. Remember how she used to stop and ask us questions?" Meg thought of something. "And she wrote our names down in that notebook of hers."

Meg had forgotten to tell Kerry about finding that book. She told her now. "It was a sort of diary," she said. "I just got to see a little of it."

The big night came. It was an elaborate party. Kathleen had followed Miss Amelia's strange conditions to the letter. Musicians came from the city, and butlers were hired to tend the door.

The orchestra played the same music played on that fateful night over sixty years before, when little Kathleen Hannigan gave her party and nobody came.

It was a stormy night, but this time everybody came. They drove through the big gates in all kinds of cars. They wore plastic raincoats to cover their costumes.

Some of the women had searched their attics for old-fashioned dresses. The men had sent to the city for high-collared suits. Some even wore wigs and false beards to get into the spirit of the affair.

Kerry's mother found a quaint old blue dress with crinoline petticoats and pantalets for Kerry to wear. Mrs. Wilson hired the dressmaker to fashion one for Meg exactly like it, in yellow.

They were bubbling with excitement when Uncle Hal came to drive them both to the party in his shining black Duesenberg. He wore a false moustache and looked very dashing and handsome.

The lights of the big house shimmered in the rain. Music poured forth into the night.

"There's Kathleen!" cried Meg when they were inside. She and Kerry had given their coats to the maid and were peeking into the ballroom.

Meg caught her breath. Kathleen was a picture. Her face was like a flower beneath her dark cloud of hair. At first Meg thought she was wearing the pink satin dress from the room upstairs. Then she saw that it was another—a new one, made just like it.

Kathleen stood near the fireplace, under the old portrait of the Hannigan children. In spite of the festive occasion, she looked nervous and frightened.

A butler was passing silver cups of punch. But the guests didn't seem to be eating or drinking. They were having a hard time dancing to the music Miss Amelia had chosen. The orchestra was playing a mournful old tune called "After the Ball." It discouraged the dancers.

Kathleen saw the girls at the door and came running to them. "Oh, I'm so glad you're here," she

129

whispered to Meg. "It's awful. Nobody knows what to do or say. And it's such a dreary night."

"Don't worry," Meg whispered back. "I'm sure the party will perk up. At least, all the people came. Now the house is yours for sure."

But the party didn't perk up—not right away. Uncle Hal had gone over to speak with Mrs. Partlow. She looked very aristocratic in her black satin gown. Their faces were serious as they looked around at the unhappy guests.

What was wrong? Meg wondered. The air felt cold and clammy. It seemed almost as if there were some dreadful spell over the room.

By now everyone knew about the death of the first Kathleen. They knew about the shameful tragedy. Had they all felt a little guilty, perhaps, even if they hadn't played a part in those tragic events of the past?

The music came to a dreary halt.

"It's *spooky*," said Kerry in Meg's ear. "I thought it would be such fun."

Meg moved toward her uncle, Kerry at her side. Uncle Hal never failed to raise her spirits. Meg pressed close to him, but he didn't even smile at her.

"It's ghastly, Harold," Mrs. Partlow said to Meg's

uncle. "Poor little Kathleen. Is this party going to be a fiasco, too—like that other one?"

Uncle Hal put his arm around his niece. "I hope not," he said. "I was sure the old house would be a happy place, now that these two young detectives have solved the riddle of the noisy ghost."

"I'm afraid the ghost of Amelia is haunting us now," said Mrs. Partlow. "Perhaps she never forgave this town, after all, for what happened to her sister."

Meg saw her uncle frown. "I don't get that feeling at all," he said slowly. "I used to meet Amelia on the street. She always ducked her head and ran. She acted more guilty than resentful. I think she meant this party as a peace offering. She's asking the town to forgive *her* for something."

Meg was looking up at her uncle. All at once it came to her: the memory of some words written long ago by a hurt and lonely older sister. *I have to address all those invitations,* Miss Amelia had written.

Meg's heart began to beat very fast. She remembered something else, too! A closed window seat that wouldn't open.

"Come with me, Kerry," she said tensely. She

gripped Kerry's arm so hard the other girl squealed.

"Where to?"

"Don't ask questions."

She pulled her friend through the crowd. In a moment, they were skipping up the stairs to old Amelia's shabby room. Once more ghostly footsteps sounded before them. This time they didn't even notice.

Meg ripped the faded chintz cushion from the window seat. She tried to lift the lid. It still didn't open—and now she saw why. It was nailed shut, and the nails had been driven down with angry blows.

Meg had to go to the kitchen for a hammer to force the chest open. It was slow work. Questions went through her mind. When she raised the window seat, what would she find? Would she find the answer to the riddle of the old house—Miss Amelia's dreadful secret?

At last the chest was open, and Meg was reaching down.

"What is it?" asked Kerry, looking over Meg's shoulder.

A bundle of envelopes had been hidden in the bottom of the chest. There must have been a hundred in all. *A hundred party invitations that were never mailed.*

Meg took one out. Her heart skipped a beat. It was addressed to her own grandmother, who had since passed away. *Margaret Walker Ashley.*

Poor, frightened Miss Amelia. She could never tell her tragic secret. In her jealousy over her popular young sister, she had deliberately failed to send the invitations.

15

IN THE SUMMERHOUSE

Triumphantly Meg and Kerry ran down the stairs and into the ballroom. In their hands were stacks of yellowed envelopes.

They went at once to Mrs. Partlow. She was the one who remembered that long-ago night. She had borne the shame of the town, for a crime it never committed.

As Mrs. Partlow looked at the envelopes, there were tears in her faded blue eyes. She read in a quivering voice the names of people now dead.

"I never quite believed it," she said to Uncle Hal. "The people of our town have always been proud, but they were never that cruel. Poor Amelia. And poor little Kathleen!"

Uncle Hal stood on one of the small chairs. He

asked for the crowd's attention. He told them what Meg and Kerry had discovered in the old chest.

Now there were pleased murmurs among the guests. A few shouts went up from the younger people. And all at once the strange party came to life.

The orchestra began to play again, this time in a faster tempo. They even slipped in a few modern dance tunes, to the delight of the young people.

Young and old, the guests began to have a wonderful time. Tray after tray of delicious food was passed around.

Kathleen's party was a success. She danced happily with Kerry's brother Bill.

Meg glanced toward the windows. "I think it's stopped raining, Kerry," she said. "Let's go out to the summerhouse."

Kerry knew what she wanted to do. In a moment they were outside, running past the majestic old pillars of the house.

The rain had stopped, but the grass was wet. They had to lift their crinoline skirts as they ran up the hill.

The moon had come out, but there were clouds of mist along the riverbank. Meg could almost imagine that she saw a slim, ghostly figure run back up the bank.

The girls pressed their ears against the wet wall of the small building. Meg could see Kerry's face in the moonlight, with its ghostly little freckles. She saw her eyes get bigger and bigger.

Yes, they could still hear the voice of little Kathleen Hannigan. But it was no longer a sobbing sound. It was more like a low, peaceful crooning.

Meg blinked her eyes.

"Boo!" Again there was a scary shout from behind them, then two laughing young voices.

Meg and Kerry turned around. It wasn't the twins this time but Kathleen Martin and Kerry's brother Bill.

"Seen any ghosts lately?" asked Bill teasingly.

"If Meg and Kerry stay on the job," said Kathleen, "there won't be any more ghosts. It's a lovely party, Meg—thanks to you and Kerry. The house is still old and shabby, but it looks happy now. I'm almost sorry to be leaving it."

Meg looked at her in dismay.

"What do you mean, Kathleen? Aren't you going to keep the house?"

"No," Kathleen said. "Mother and I have decided

137

to go back home in a few days. We belong in California. And mother has to get back to her teaching job."

"Kathleen has been talking with Mrs. Partlow," said Bill. "Mrs. Partlow wants to raise the money and buy the Hannigan mansion for a historical museum."

He smiled at Kathleen. "I think it's a great idea," he said. "And Kathleen can come back for the dedication, after her house has been restored."

"They are going to call it the Kathleen Hannigan Museum," said Kathleen softly. "I think Aunt Amelia would be happy about that, don't you, Meg?"

Meg nodded her head. "It's a great idea," she agreed.

She looked wistfully at her friend Kerry. They were both wondering the same thing.

Would the ghost of little Kathleen ever again be seen running near the summerhouse?

Probably not, thought Meg. *Now she can rest.*